Charlotte and The White Horse

by Ruth Krauss

pictures by Maurice Sendak

HarperCollins – New York

Charlotte
and The White Horse

This is the song of Charlotte
and Milky Way, her horse.
He was born in a stable.

He's just a colt
—I should hope so—
nothing but a colt
— not a lion, not a fire engine—

Look, he can't stand yet, his
legs wobble, look

—the winter is going,

the wind and the rains are gone
the grass is coming out of the ground
the leaves are coming out of the trees

the people are coming out of doors
they are coming out of windows
they are coming out and planting radishes,
the worms are coming out of the old apples.
— the time of my singing is come.

Arise, my love, my fair one
my milk white Milky Way—
Come away, Pure White,
All White and Strong
—stronger than Hero the Great Dog
—sure, but he couldn't wag his tail like Hero—

At first he could not even stand.

But then he does. Oh yes, he did
—he is ready.
He looks around and sees a little girl smiling.

Then a big man comes, who is her father, and says,
he won't make a good race horse so we will sell him.
Then Nathan can go to college when he is grown.
—That's the little brother.
Now just sorrow is coming in
Now just sorrow is coming in

Oh Daddy, please, she begs, let me keep him.
I will take care of him. Oh, Daddy, please.

And he did.
And she did.
And they became as one.

And everybody comes and celebrates and birds
are flying in the air and
the tender grape gives a good smell,

the flowers appear on the earth

Then the multitude gather and sing
Happy Birthday, dear Milky Way,
and when he hears his given name for the first time
the tears come up in his eyes
and they run down streaking his face
and they run down the face, too, of Charlotte,
the only one, nevermore a lonely one

— and ever after, every morning,
she groomed him and they went for a gallop
and in the evening,

she tucked him in and said goodnight.
And she always remembered—she never forgot—
to leave him water to drink
and some hay and some oats because

horses eat all night when they're not sleeping.